D1083100

The Giant Vegetable Garden

by
Nadine Bernard Westcott

An Atlantic Monthly Press Book
Boston   Little, Brown and Company   Toronto

FIRST EDITION

Library of Congress Cataloging in Publication Data

Westcott, Nadine Bernard.
   The giant vegetable garden.

   "An Atlantic Monthly Press book."
   SUMMARY: In their desire to win the prize for
finest vegetables at the fair, the townspeople let
their gardens grow until the plants threaten to
strangle the village.
   [1. Vegetables — Fiction] I. Title.
PZ7.W51963Gi   [E]   80-29261
ISBN 0-316-93129-2
ISBN 0-316-93130-6 (pbk.)

HO

Published simultaneously in Canada
by Little, Brown & Company (Canada) Limited

PRINTED IN THE UNITED STATES OF AMERICA

For Becky and Wendy

ATLANTIC-LITTLE, BROWN BOOKS
ARE PUBLISHED BY
LITTLE, BROWN AND COMPANY
IN ASSOCIATION WITH
THE ATLANTIC MONTHLY PRESS

It was spring in Peapack.
The mayor called a meeting of the town.
"Contest at the county fair!" he shouted.
"And a cash prize to the town that
grows the finest vegetables!"
When he said "prize," everyone was quiet.
Then a murmur went through the crowd:
"A prize! A prize!"

"All in favor of entering, say Aye."
"Aye!" shouted all the people,
for it was not a rich town and
already they were dreaming of the prize.
"But what will we do with the money?"
asked a young boy.
"Divide it!" boomed the mayor,
and that was that.

Everyone set to work
digging and planting,
watering and weeding,
until soon the vegetables grew
plump and ready to be picked.

7

"It's time to pick!" said the children,
holding up a bright red tomato.
"No!" boomed the mayor.
"Prize vegetables must be bigger yet!
All in favor of winning?" he asked.

"Aye!" shouted all the people.
(Everyone had a plan for the prize.)
"Wait then," said the mayor.
"I will tell you when to pick!"
And they all went back to work.

Every day they watered and weeded,
dusted and sprayed,
waxed and polished.

The ladies cooed at the cauliflowers
and sang to the beets,
and the more they talked to them
the larger their vegetables grew.
They grew and grew and grew.

And so did everyone's dreams of winning.

Up shot the vines,
higher than the houses —
over the rooftops and into the streets.

But still the mayor waited.
He watched and waited,
waited and watched,
for he had his dreams too.
Finally he could wait no longer.
"Pick!" he yelled. "Everyone pick!"

The finest vegetables were carefully picked and packed for the county fair.

Everyone argued over
who would accept the prize.
"I will!" said the mayor,
and that was that.

That night everyone dreamed about the prize.

And in the morning they
pushed and shoved when their town won.

But when the prize was divided,
and divided again,
and again,
no one was any richer than before.

The poor town was a tangle
of tomatoes and squash,
peas and pumpkins and corn.
What could be done?

The children had an idea.
"That's it! That's it!" cried the mayor.

"Bring hammers and nails, hatchets and saws,
quilts and needles and thread. Everyone,
bring oil and vinegar."

They chopped and cut,
sawed and stacked,

rinsed and scrubbed
and dried.
Sliced,

jarred,
cooked and labeled
to pack away for winter.

23

From the strawberries
they made fresh jam
and a giant strawberry pie.

25

Then, high on the hill,
they made a salad

and had a picnic

complete with watermelon and strawberry pie.

And then the little village rested peacefully . . .

until the next town meeting.

"Contest at the county fair!" shouted the mayor.

"And a cash prize to the town that grows
the finest flowers!"